For my patchwork family

First published in the United States, Great Britain, Canada, Australia, and New Zealand in 2013 by NorthSouth Books Inc.,
an imprint of NordSüd Verlag AG, CH-8005 Zürich, Switzerland.

Distributed in the United States by NorthSouth Books Inc., New York 10016.
Library of Congress Cataloging-in-Publication Data is available.

ISBN: 978-0-7358-4149-9
Printed in Germany by Grafisches Centrum Cuno GmbH & Co. KG, 39240 Calbe, June 2013.
1 3 5 7 9 • 10 8 6 4 2

www.northsouth.com

Ute Krause

No Ordinary Family

North
South

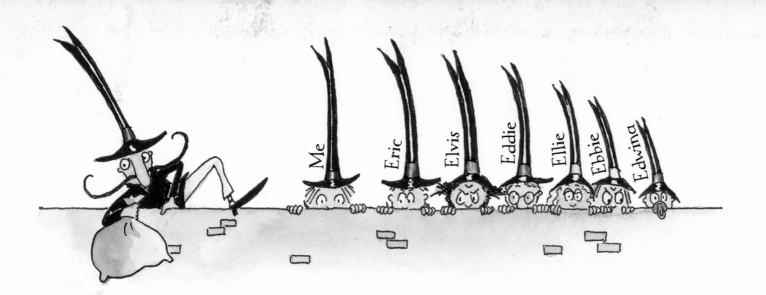

I have a really big family. There are about 9 to 22 of us . . . depending on the day.

This is my dad. He's a bandit. Each week me and my bandit siblings—Eric, Elvis, Eddie, Ellie, Ebbie, and Edwina—help him work. When we're done helping, we pack our bags and make sure that Edwina has her pacifier. Then we visit Mom.

It wasn't always this way.

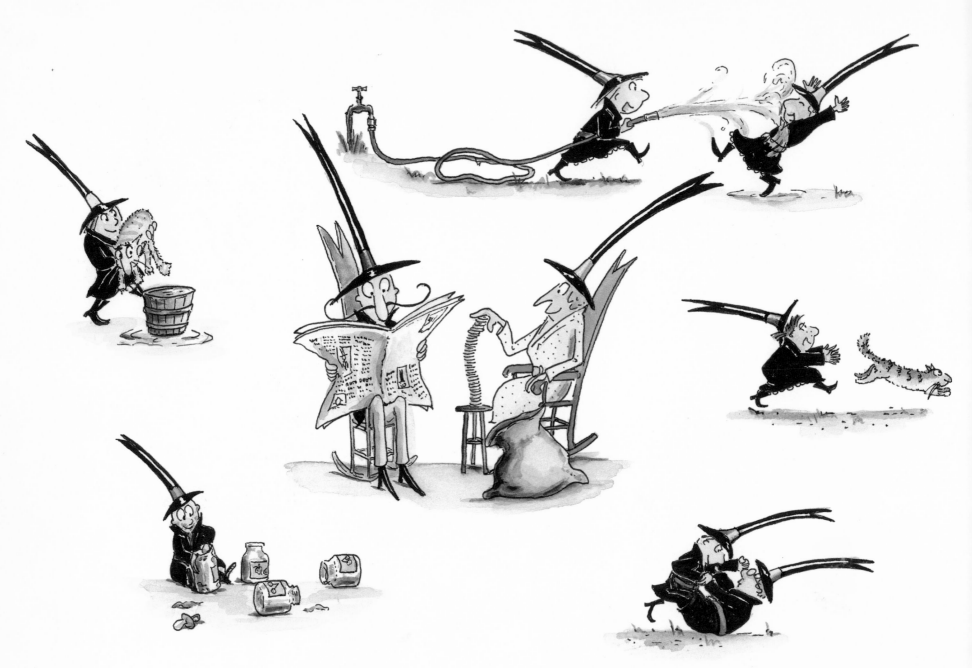

In the beginning, we were a very ordinary family—
even for bandits.

Then one day Mom and Dad invented a new game. Except it wasn't a game. They were having a little disagreement—and it wasn't about which bank to rob.

They just weren't getting along . . .

. . . until one day Dad moved out.

   We missed him terribly. Without Dad, life was
only half the fun.

   So we packed our bags, made sure Edwina had
her pacifier, then went to visit Dad.

   And from that day on we traveled back and forth
with our little suitcases.

But one day things were different. A princess
and her children had come to stay with Dad.
They were the most prim and prissy little
princes and princesses I had ever seen!

It was going to be the worst day ever—until
Eddie had a great idea.

"Psst! When are they leaving?"
I whispered to Dad.

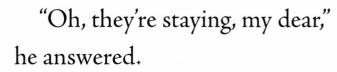

"Oh, they're staying, my dear,"
he answered.
"They're part of the family now."

And stay they did.
After that we had two of everything:
two sets of Christmases . . .

two sets of birthday parties . . .

two sets of plates . . .

two sets of toothbrushes . . .

and two sets of rules.

two sets of beds . . .

Back and forth we traveled—a few days with Mom, a few days with Dad.

It was hard at first. Sometimes Mom and Dad argued. Sometimes Dad and the princess argued.

Sometimes Mom was sad.

Sometimes Dad was sad.

And sometimes even the princess
was sad.

So were we. We wanted to have Dad to ourselves.
But he was never alone. The princess and her
children were always there.

"I wish it was like in the old days,"
said Emma. "Things were so
much better then."

I agreed. Then I had
a great idea.

In the dark of the night, we crept into the princes'
and princesses' bedroom and set free little field mice we'd
found in the forest. The mice ran around wildly until
the little royals screamed and jumped and . . .

. . . ran into the woods as fast as their legs could carry them.

The princess ran after them. We rubbed our hands in glee.

"Hurray! Alone at last!"

"Now everything will be back to normal," Emma said happily.

Boy, were we wrong! Dad was quite upset that his princess was gone. Nobody could cheer him up, not even little Edwina. Perhaps my idea wasn't so great after all.

There was no one to tease and no one to annoy. To be honest, it was boring. Dad stayed in bed the entire day. Not even a good bank robbery could tempt him.

So we decided to go
find them. We crept
through dark woods,
searched every corner and
crevice and every nook
and cranny until at last . . .

... we found them!

The princess and her children were stuck in a swamp! Of course, we pulled them out. They were so happy to see us, they didn't even care about the mice.

Dad was thrilled to have us all back and even more
thrilled that we were getting along. Dad had enough
love in his heart for all of us.

Then Mom announced that she'd met someone special:
a really cool dragon with 5 dragon children of his own.
So now there are 22 of us—16 people and 6 dragons.

We're anything but ordinary . . . and we couldn't be
happier about it.

We all get along so well that Mom and Dad
moved a little closer to each other.

Now we throw wild parties, and sometimes,
if they're lucky, we even invite the grown-ups.